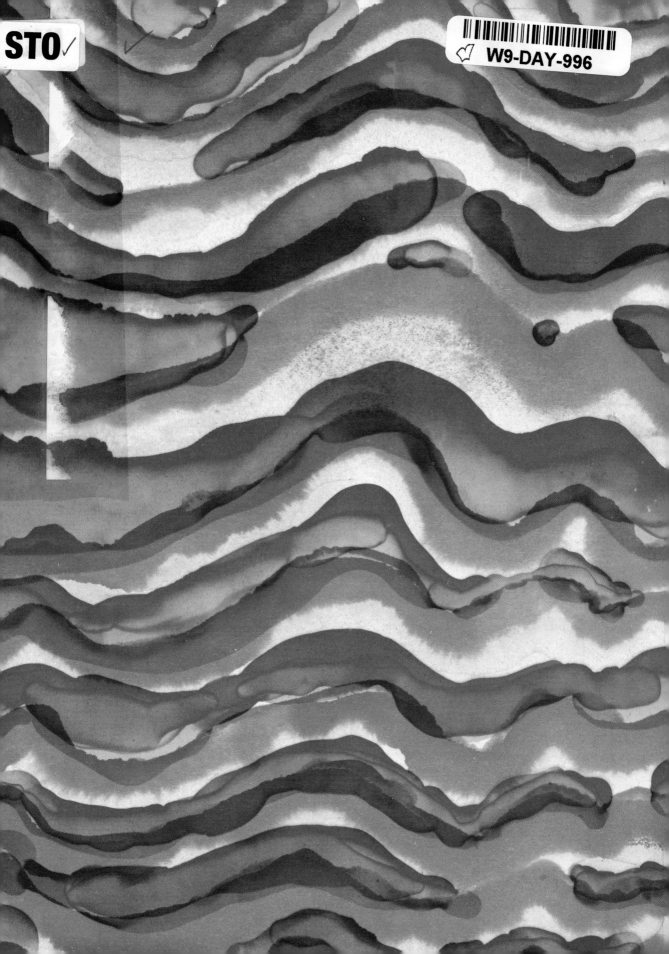

MERMAID OF STORMS

story by Mary Calhoun
pictures by Janet McCaffery

William Morrow & Company
New York 1970

The mermaid lived in the deeps of the sea,
edge of the sea, surf of the sea,
the mermaid and her sisters.
Singing and swinging
in the vines of the sea,
the mermaid and her sisters
bubbled the water with laughter,
rippled it with their tails.

She was the smallest mermaid,
and her name was Carita,
which means "little dear."
But she was the mermaid
who made storms with her comb and her tail.
Whenever she sat on a rock on the shore
and combed her hair,
the wind began to push the waves.
As she swished her tail in the water,
the waves piled higher.
Laughing and swishing,
she swirled up a stormy sea,
then riffled it smooth again with her tail.
And her sisters sang with joy.
For a mermaid's delight is a stormy sea.
Then mermaids dance on the waves,
singing and tossing their hair in the wind.

One day her sisters begged Carita
to make a special storm,
so the small mermaid soared upward
and burst into sunlight.
Shaking the sea spray from her hair,
she swam to her favorite rock on the shore.
There she ran her comb
through her long hair
and swayed her tail in the tide.
The waves began to tip and curl
and reach toward the wind,
and the wind began to bring in clouds.
But then the mermaid heard a fluting sound.
The sound sang over the sea,
and the water was smooth again.
Looking down the beach,
Carita saw a boy sitting on the next rock.
He was breathing on a fluted shell,
and his shell music was calming the sea.

Carita tucked her comb in her hair
and swam down to the boy.
"Stop that fluting!" she cried.
"I'm trying to make a stormy sea."
The boy grinned. "I know," he said.
"And I'm stopping you.
My father is a fisherman,
and he and his friends
are out in their boats on the water.
If you make a storm, they might drown."
"Drown? What is that?" asked Carita.
For the mermaid had lived forever.
"What is that to me?
My sisters are waiting."
Flouncing her tail,
the mermaid began to comb her hair
and ripple up the sea.

But the boy, whose name was Pedro,
hummed on his shell,
smoothing the waves again.
Carita combed faster
and churned her tail in the waves.
And her combing and swishing were stronger
than the magic of the singing shell.
Pedro called, "Say, mermaid,
come play with me!
I'll show you how
to build a sand castle,
because you're so pretty.
Or don't mermaids like to play?"
Carita shook her hair.
"You silly two-legged fish!
Of course, mermaids play!
But I play with the sea."

Still, she liked to hear she was pretty,
so she stayed on the beach with the boy.
Pedro and Carita
mounded wet sand into a castle.
They made towers and tunnels
and little peepholes.
Carita lay on her stomach,
fluttering her tail in the tide,
as she shaped the sand castle,
and she hummed with the fun of it.
She'd never thought
of building a castle with sand.
She peeped through a hole
at Pedro's bright eye and laughed.
"I see you!" they both said.

Carita dove under the waves
and brought up shells from the sea floor,
bright coral, pink-rippled shells
and pearls.
Singing softly, she showed Pedro
how to make a shell castle
with periwinkle spires
and pearls for windows.
"Beautiful!" they both said,
as they looked at
the two castles they'd made.
But when Carita's back was turned,
Pedro slipped the comb from her hair
and placed it and his singing shell
on a rock far up the beach from the water.
Yet Pedro liked the small mermaid.
"Come see my secret pool," he asked her.
They went around the curve of the shore,
the boy wading,
the mermaid sliding in the tide,
and came to a tidewater pool in the rocks.

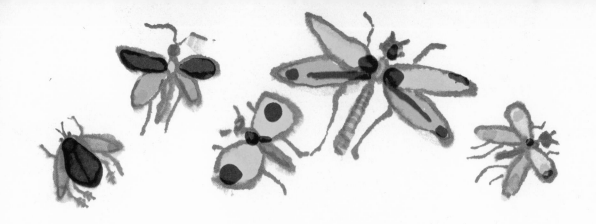

Sea urchins and sea anemone
rimmed the pool like flowers.
"Just the place for me!" cried Carita.
She splashed into the pool
and floated in the middle,
a mermaid's pool edged with sea flowers.
"I have a secret place, too," Carita said,
"and I'll show you."
Swimming at the edge of the rocks,
she led Pedro through an arch,
into a sea cave.
Green sea light shimmered on the walls,
reflecting the water.
"It's an echo cave," Carita whispered.
"Hoo!" she called,
and "Hoo!" came back
from the walls of the cave.
"Me!" Pedro shouted.
"Me!" said the cave.

Carita and Pedro
went back to their castles,
and Pedro gathered sand dollars
to make a necklace for the mermaid.
But just then voices shrieked
from the breakers out to sea.
There on the crest of the waves
rose a flurry of mermaids.
"A storm, Carita!" cried the mermaids.
"You promised!"

Carita laughed. "A storm, of course!
The best play of all!"
She reached for her comb,
and she found it was gone.
Wide-eyed, she looked at the boy.
Pedro hung his head. "I took it," he said.
"Give it back!" cried the mermaid.
The boy shook his head. "I can't.
Not until my father's boat comes in."
Carita saw her comb lying on the rock
far across the sand.
Flinging herself up on her tail,
she tried to run to it,
but her tail slid out from under her.
The small mermaid fell on the sand
and began to cry.
"Give me my comb," she wailed.
How terrible,
never to be able to make a storm again!
Her sisters would tear out her hair.

"Please," begged Carita.
"If you'll fetch my comb,
I'll tell you the secret of egg water."
Pedro only laughed.
"We throw out the water
eggs are boiled in," he said.
"Fool!" She looked at him scornfully.
"The secret of egg water
is the secret of life."
The sea stayed smooth, the sky blue.
The waves purred,
but the mermaids shrieked and swam closer.
"Then I'll give you a purse!"
Carita cried.
"The purse will always hold a gold coin,
no matter how many times you spend it."
The boy looked out to sea
and shook his head.
"No," he said.
"My father might drown."
The sea stayed smooth, the sky dark blue.
The waves purred,
but the mermaids shrieked and swam closer.

"Then we'll sing up a sea dance for you,"
whispered Carita.
She began to sing,
and her sisters sang with her.
Up on their tails,
in the white-curling waves,
the mermaids danced and sang.
They sang with such gayness
that even the fish danced,
flipping their tails
and jumping out of the water.

"Come dance with me," sang Carita to Pedro.
Sliding into the water,
she pulled the boy with her.
"Dance!" shrieked the mermaid's sisters.
"Dance forever
until you give back the comb!"
But Pedro stumbled in the surf,
and waves flowed over his head.
He came up choking, his nose full of water.
"I'll drown," he gasped.
Then Carita understood what drowning meant,
and she was sorry for what she'd done.
Swimming, she pulled the boy
back to the shore.
"I'm sorry!" she cried.
"So I'll give you a promise."
The small mermaid
whispered at the edge of the sea.

"Not you, not your father,
not one of your family shall ever drown."
"Ho!" Pedro shouted.
"Then I'll give back your comb."
He ran across the sand
and brought the comb to the mermaid,
where she floated in the tide.
He smiled at her
as she tucked the comb in her hair.
"Many thanks for your gift,
for your promise," Pedro said.
"Many thanks for my comb!"
said the mermaid, laughing.
"I'll come again to build castles."

Soon the fishing boats appeared,
heading for harbor,
the boy's father home safe from the sea.
Then Carita began to call up a storm.
She sat on her rock
and combed down her hair,
while she stroked the sea with her tail.
The waves ruffled
and rose into white-crashing peaks.
The wind rushed black clouds over the sea.

"A storm! A storm!"
cried the mermaid's sisters.
Gliding on their tails,
they rose to frolic on the windblown waves.
Singing, hair streaming,
the mermaids danced
in the dash and tumble and spray.
And then Carita swam out to her sisters,
to dance in the storm on the top of the sea.